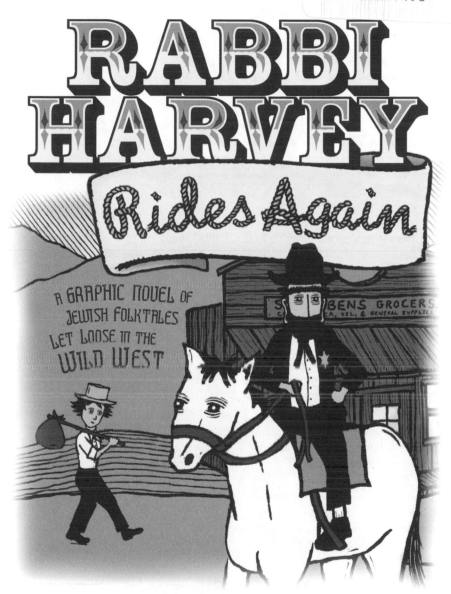

RABBI HARVEY
Rides Again

A GRAPHIC NOVEL OF JEWISH FOLKTALES LET LOOSE IN THE WILD WEST

STEVE SHEINKIN

For People of All Faiths, All Backgrounds

JEWISH LIGHTS Publishing

www.jewishlights.com

Rabbi Harvey Rides Again:
A Graphic Novel of Jewish Wisdom Let Loose in the Wild West

2015 PJ Library Quality Paperback Edition

Library of Congress Cataloging-in-Publication Data
Available upon request.

   ISBN-13: 978-1-58023- 347-7 (quality pbk.)
   ISBN-10: 1-58023-347-3 (quality pbk.)
   ISBN-13: 978-1-68442-258-6 (PJ Library pbk)

Manufactured in the United States of America
Cover design: Jenny Buono, based on a design created by Sara Dismukes
Cover art: Stephen Sheinkin

For People of All Faiths, All Backgrounds
Published by Jewish Lights Publishing
An Imprint of Turner Publishing Company
4507 Charlotte Avenue, Suite 100
Nashville, TN 37209
Tel: (615) 255-2665
www.jewishlights.com

CONTENTS

INTRODUCTION

It's an awkward thing, writing for a character who is much smarter than I am. In the year and half since *The Adventures of Rabbi Harvey: A Graphic Novel of Jewish Wisdom and Wit in the Wild West* (Jewish Lights) was published, people have asked me for the Rabbi's advice on all kinds of ethical, personal, and even political dilemmas. My answers never seem to satisfy. To be honest, I really don't know how he would bring peace to the Middle East.

Luckily, Rabbi Harvey hardly relies on me for his wisdom. As in the first volume of Harvey's adventures, *Rabbi Harvey Rides Again: A Graphic Novel of Jewish Wisdom Let Loose in the Wild West* combines and adapts stories and insights from classic Jewish folktales, Hasidic legends, and Talmudic teachings. The stories are set in the fictional town of Elk Spring, Colorado, high in the Rocky Mountains. Part old world rabbi, part Wild West sheriff, Harvey protects his town and delivers justice wielding only the weapons of wisdom, kindness, and humor.

A few characters from volume one reappear here, including Harvey's nemesis, "Big Milt" Wasserman, the hands-down favorite of kids I've met at schools and book stores. We also hear again from my personal favorite villain, the town's sweet-faced *bubbe* gone horribly wrong. A new character—the luckless gold miner named Abigail—was inspired by the concerns of several people, most importantly my wife, Rachel, that Harvey seemed a bit lonely. A woman from France emailed me a possible solution, saying, "I confess, I'm in love with the Rabbi!" But I thought it might be more practical to introduce someone a bit closer to 1870s Colorado. So that's where Abigail comes in. We'll see where it goes.

For Rachel's countless suggestions, for her almost absurd insistence (in the face of years of publishers' rejections) that the first Rabbi Harvey book would one day find a home, and for coming up with the title of this new volume—for all that and much more—this book is for her.

ABIGAIL v. THE WIND

In an icy creek, a mile and a half high in the Rocky Mountains ...

... a few stubborn miners were panning for gold.

Most of the miners had moved on to other mountains, to other streams and rivers. And with good reason.

There really did not seem to be any gold left in this creek.

Nothing.

But Abigail decided to give it a few more weeks. She did not have enough money to start over somewhere new.

No way I go back East empty-handed.

Two more luckless weeks passed.

Then it started to rain.

Perfect.

The rain poured down day after day. Abigail soon ran out of food.

But not water.

The sun finally came out the next morning.

But Abigail was in no mood to pan for gold. She was furious with the wind for stealing her bread. She wanted justice.

So she packed up her things and set out to find a judge who would hear her case.

She walked for days, several times nearly fainting from hunger.

A farmer gave her an apple, and some advice on where she might bring her case.

Sounds like a job for Rabbi Harvey.

Who's he?

As the farmer explained, Rabbi Harvey was well known throughout the Rocky Mountain region for his wisdom and fairness. Abigail headed toward the town of Elk Spring, Colorado, where the Rabbi lived.

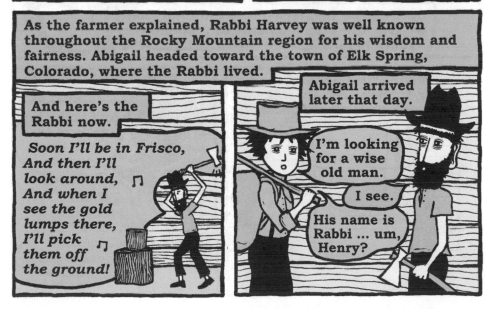

And here's the Rabbi now.

Soon I'll be in Frisco, And then I'll look around, And when I see the gold lumps there, I'll pick them off the ground!

Abigail arrived later that day.

I'm looking for a wise old man.

I see.

His name is Rabbi ... um, Henry?

Hm ... I know of a fairly young, somewhat intelligent rabbi named Harvey.

I guess that'll have to do.

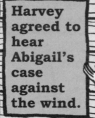

Harvey agreed to hear Abigail's case against the wind.

And then the wind came in, without knocking, *like this!* And stole my last loaf of bread!

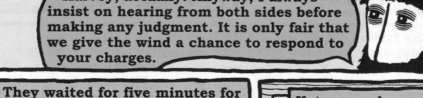

Interesting. You have a very strong case.

Thanks, Henry.

Harvey, actually. Anyway, I always insist on hearing from both sides before making any judgment. It is only fair that we give the wind a chance to respond to your charges.

They waited for five minutes for the wind. Then ten minutes.

Show your face, you coward.

Not even a breeze.

Any thoughts on how to rule here, Harv?

I think punishing the wind is well beyond your jurisdiction.

Startled by the voice, Harvey swung a bit wildly.

I believe this is yours.

Thank you.

My name is Morris, Rabbi. I understand you're the man to talk to around here.

Depends what you want to talk about.

I have a very large sum of money I wish to give to a worthy cause.

I'll see what I can do.

The man opened his bag and took out a metal box, heavy with coins.

There's well over a hundred dollars in here, Rabbi.

Sweet *bubbe.*

I am a merchant, Rabbi, fairly successful I suppose. Anyway, a few days ago I was on my way to Santa Fe to buy a few goods.

Fascinating, fascinating.... I'll bet it looks charming on her.

Well, this has been a most pleasant chat, but now I must be going.

Please give my best to your wife, and have a nice day.

But the thief was as sharp as a new sewing needle.

Thanks, pal. Now, hand over your money.

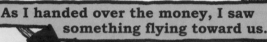

As I handed over the money, I saw something flying toward us.

What in the world is that?

The thief thought it was another trick.

Nice try, friend.

It's right behind you!

I'd like to put this robbery behind me, pal. So hand over your watch and I'll be—

The flying object smacked right into the thief's head, knocking him out cold.

That was remarkable.

WASSERMAN AND SON, ~~BARBERS~~ OUTLAWS

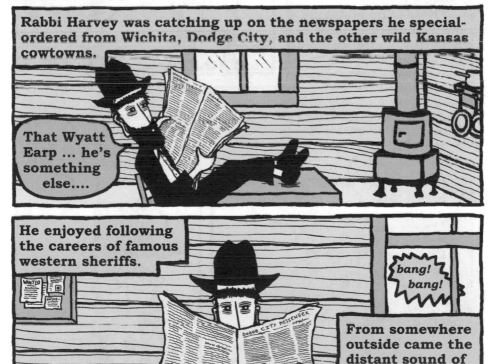

The gunshots sounded like they were getting closer.

bang! bang, bang!

The story is so well written, I can almost hear the gunfire.

Very soon a bullet crashed through the window of Harvey's office.

Perhaps I had better investigate.

As Rabbi Harvey was about to find out, the men doing the shooting were Milton "Big Milt" Wasserman, and his son, Wolfie Wasserman—

currently the most feared father-and-son outlaw team west of Kansas City.

You better believe it.

Many years ago, Big Milt and his gang had ruled the town of Elk Spring.

The people there really loved me, Wolfie.

Who wouldn't love you, Pops?

Excellent point.

But then Rabbi Harvey came along, and ruined everything.

After getting booted out of Elk Spring, Milt decided to go straight. He opened a traveling barber business, and taught his son to cut hair and shave beards.

WASSERM & SON BARBER

But Milt was unsatisfied with the money.

Hold still, buddy.

You can't get rich on fifty cents for a cut and shave.

So Milt taught his son to steal instead. They rode around the West, robbing stores and banks.

Come to Papa!

HARDWARE & MINERS SUPPLIES

WASS & BA

This proved to be much more profitable.

Smart kid.

Now Big Milt was looking for a new town to bleed dry. And, perhaps, to settle an old score.

Today, Wolfie, I teach you how to take over a town.

Sounds good, Pops.

TOWN OF ELK SPRING

Milt and Wolfie strolled down the street and into the saloon.

bang!

bang!

I wonder what Wyatt Earp would do? I suppose he would shoot them. Perhaps I'll try a different approach.

Big Milt and Wolfie moved into the rooms above the saloon.

How much per night?

One dollar, sir.

How 'bout none dollars?

Well ...

Deal.

And you get to live.

They took supplies from stores in town. They ordered huge meals at Sara's Cafe. Wolfie especially loved the pancakes.

Can't you cook 'em any faster?

They paid for nothing.

They went anywhere they pleased in town.

So how are we doing on the long division? Who can tell me the answer to the first problem?

Right here! I know!

Oh, please don't let her call on me ...

Yes, Noah?

4,521

Very good.

No fair, I knew that.

Lucky guess, kid.

That night, in the saloon:

SAL

... so Abraham Lincoln is sitting in this restaurant, see? And he takes a sip from his cup, and winces.

He puts the cup back down on the saucer. The waitress asks if he would like anything else.

And Old Abe nods slowly and says—

Harvey did not get the straight.

After losing his food money for the week, he walked to the wagon and took a pair of scissors.

The next day he walked back to the restaurant to return the scissors.

Milt and Wolfie were enjoying another free meal when the Rabbi arrived.

Another bucket of syrup!

Here are the scissors, Milton.

Thanks, Rebbe.

You sure you cut anything?

Anyway, sorry to interrupt again, but I noticed you have a nice pocket watch there. Any chance I could borrow it just for tonight?

This here's a solid gold watch, Rabbi.

I'd only need it for a few hours.

I'm always overcooking my corn bread.

That's the worst.

It gets very dry.

Milt thought it over.

He agreed to lend Harvey his gold pocket watch.

The next morning, at the restaurant:

Good morning, gentlemen. Here is your watch, Big Milt.

And here's another gold watch.

Another one?

Yes, it seems that yours had a baby overnight. So naturally the newborn belongs to you.

Naturally.

You look just like your mother.

What's going on here, Pops?

Why worry, Son? Are we or are we not making a nice profit?

Harvey started toward the door, but then turned back toward the table.

Oh, I almost forgot. Could I perhaps borrow one of your firearms?

You mean a gun, Rabbi?

Yes, a friend of mine is having a terrible problem with rats in his barn. I don't feel quite right about shooting at them, but in all fairness they do seem to have eaten a significant portion of his beet harvest.

I'd bring it right back. The gun, that is.

Milt did some quick math.

You sure you need only one gun, Rabbi?

Yes, I imagine so. Unless ... do you think the job might go faster with two guns?

Milt convinced the Rabbi to take his gun, and Wolfie's too.

LADIES SHOES & SLIPPERS

GROCERIES FLOUR, OIL, etc.

RUSSELMAN'S GENERAL MERCHANDISE

HIMROO & GAT LEATHER BOOT

Harvey returned to his office.

That night, in the saloon:

Pour me another, bud. And pour one for yourself.

You know, I'm as excited as I was the night my son here was born.

Wolfie, go look again and see if the Rabbi is coming.

Sure, Pops.

But the Rabbi never came.

It's ... there was a terrible tragedy. I'm afraid, late last night ... your guns passed away.

They *what*?

Both of 'em?

I did everything I could, I assure you, but ... I just couldn't save them.

They were buried early this morning.

That's completely absurd, Rabbi! How can guns die?

You seemed ready enough to accept that the scissors and gold watch gave birth.

So why are you surprised

that a gun can die?

Big Milt was beat. And he knew it.

Mental note: Leave town. Never return.

I feel bad we missed the funeral, Pops.

Don't say another word about it, Son.

Ever. To anyone. Get it?

Got it.

Good.

Milt and Wolfie packed up later that morning, got in their wagon, and headed west.

Maybe we could charge sixty cents for a cut and shave.

They decided to take another crack at the traveling barber business.

Grass grew over the burial site.

THE RABBI'S NEW SUIT

Every few years, Rabbi Harvey went to his favorite tailor's shop in Denver to buy a new suit.

Have you heard the story about King Solomon and the tailor?

Only about a million times, Rabbi.

When the suit was ready, Harvey asked the tailor to wrap it up carefully. He did not want it to get dirty during his long journey home.

L.M. BARTLES CO.

EN PRINTING COMPANY.

WHOLESALE G
DOORS, PAINTS, OILS

GROCERY & LIQUORS.

LUMBER, GLAS

ACOWARE & STOVE

Harvey dropped the suit off at his hotel.

Now, for something to eat.

As I was saying, that railroad bill will never get out of committee without more support from the administration.

Yes, I very much agree.

Harvey spotted a waiter with a platter of food. He was interested.

Howdy, sir. What have you got there?

Smoked trout with honey dill mustard.

The waiter turned and walked away.

Sounds good.

Meanwhile, at a table nearby:

So true, Governor.

So right, so wise.

Harvey saw an empty seat at the table.

Greetings, Governor. Is there room for one more?

The governor and his guests looked up at Harvey.

Sorry, bud.

Moments later:

HAPPY BIRTHDAY
TERRITORIAL GOVERNOR

I can't believe I voted for that guy.

Harvey went back to his hotel and changed into his new suit.

Not bad...

Then he walked to the hotel.

FEDERAL BANK
DEPOSITORY & SAFET

And returned to the party.

THE TREASURE UNDER THE PICKLES

Harris had the dream again. It was the fifth night in a row.

He found himself in the city of Denver — a place he had never actually been.

He walked into a general store, pushed aside a barrel of pickles, and began prying up the floor boards.

And there, beneath the floor, he found a priceless treasure.

crack

The next morning he told his wife about the dream.

... and there it was again, Mina, a priceless treasure!

You have to admit, we could certainly use a priceless treasure.

Harris, we could certainly use fifty cents.

True.

Harris walked on and soon came to a general store.

This must be the place.

He stepped inside, took out his hammer, and looked around.

It was right about here in the dream. I'll have to move this pickle barrel. I'm just a bit concerned ... if I begin digging a hole, won't someone notice? Well, I'll just have to work quickly.

He shoved aside the pickles and went to work.

crack

Looking for something?

Not especially. Why do you ask?

I couldn't help but notice that you were attempting to remove the floor.

Harris tried to think fast.

This was not his specialty.

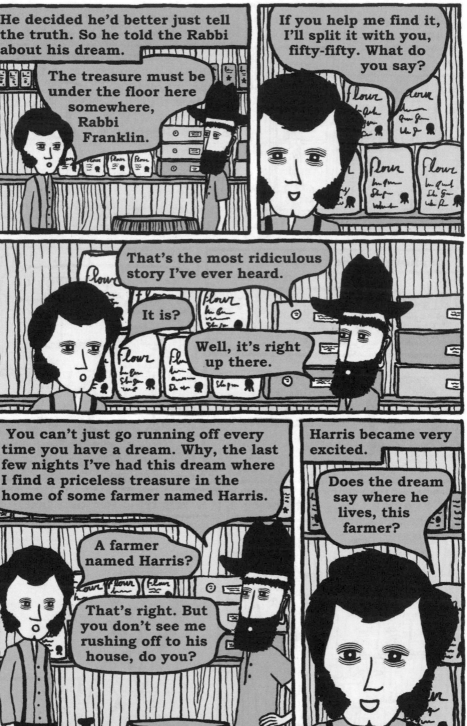

Harris ran to his farm and started looking around.

Where should I begin my search?

He went into the house, and looked behind the stove. He searched under the bed. He checked under the table.

Where could the treasure be hidden? I should have asked that rabbi for more specific directions.

Suddenly he heard strange sounds coming from the chimney.

scrape, scrape

conk!

Ah-ha!

He quickly crawled over to investigate.

Is that you, treasure?

?

Never mind the sweet talk, Harris. Just get me out of here!

THE LEADVILLE SCAVENGER HUNT

It was that time of year again — time for the annual Rocky Mountain Rabbi Convention. This year's event was held in the town of Leadville, Colorado.

The convention featured workshops, talks, and debates. But for Harvey, it was mainly an opportunity to hang out with other rabbis and, with any luck, to catch a few trout.

WELCOME RABBIS

On the last day of the convention, the hosts announced a surprise contest.

Rabbi Marcus and Rosa, his wife, explained the rules.

You have eight hours to locate the most valuable item you can find. It can be absolutely anything.

Whoever brings back the most precious item will be the winner.

You have until five o'clock tonight. Starting ... now!

The rabbis rushed out and began searching.

The most valuable item ... what can I find?

Rabbi Harvey had an idea.

I should have just enough time to get there and back.

He reached his destination a little after noon.

Inside the hut.

I was, *pant, pant* ... wondering, *pant* ...

Catch your breath, Harvey.

Up ahead, around a bend in the road, a thief stood waiting. He saw a traveler coming toward him.

About time.

And he looks like an easy one, too.

The thief jumped out into the road.

Stick 'em up, pal!

Hand over your valuables! And make it fast!

WELCOME RABBIS

Back in Leadville, the rabbis were returning to the convention hall with the items they had found.

Two more minutes, gentlemen.

The rabbis began presenting their entries to the judges.

This is a Kiddush cup from—

Another one?

Please note the fine craftsmanship.

The thief blasted two quick shots through my jacket.

bang!

bang!

That's very accurate shooting. Simply remarkable.

It's what I do.

You must be very proud.

With masterful aim like that, you could probably shoot right through my shirt. When my friend sees how close I came to getting killed, he'll be too worried to get upset with me for losing his stupid candlestick.

rip!

bang!

Luckily, I am fairly slender.

Now, about that candlestick.

Oh, I'm afraid I couldn't possibly give it to you.

You forget, I've got the gun.

No, I haven't forgotten. But I doubt your gun will do you much good, now that it's out of bullets.

How's this for no bullets?

bang!

And that makes six shots. Now, please correct me if I'm mistaken, but I believe that Schofield Model 3 of yours holds six bullets.

I was not mistaken.

click, click, click

The thief reached into his pocket for more bullets. But I charged at him and knocked him down. I'm stronger than I look.

Apparently.

I've got this thing won.

This is all highly interesting, Rabbi, but what exactly does it have to do with the empty wine bottle?

That wine bottle holds my entry in the contest.

You see, after our brief struggle, the thief and I got to talking.

I never set out to become a thief, Rabbi.

I believe you, Fred.

My mother always hoped I'd become a dentist. We used to stay up late reading medical books, and she would quiz me on all the stuff that can go wrong with your teeth and gums.

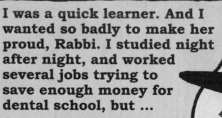

I was a quick learner. And I wanted so badly to make her proud, Rabbi. I studied night after night, and worked several jobs trying to save enough money for dental school, but ...

Other expenses always seemed to come up, and the months and years were passing by.

I tried one small robbery, just for money for school. And one theft led to another, and ... what would she think if she could see me now? I'm, *sniff*, so ashamed....

You're still a young man.

The man sat on the fallen tree, crying like a child, vowing he would never steal again, vowing to begin a new life.

A large tear pooled in the corner of his eye and slipped down his cheek, and at that moment I grabbed an empty wine bottle from my pack, held it to his face, and caught the tear.

That is my entry in the contest — the thief's tear of repentance.

The judges seemed impressed.

The whole room was silent.

Rabbi Harvey was awarded first prize.

WELCOME RABBIS

STUMP THE RABBI

I've always dreamed of being rich, Rabbi. Think I'm there yet?

Perhaps. How much money do you have?

Well over a hundred thousand dollars.

Do you want more?

Of course.

You're not rich.

Next!

It was time again for the Elk Spring Fair. As usual, the "Stump the Rabbi" booth drew the largest crowds. For five cents, you got to ask Rabbi Harvey one question.

So I know I'm a fool, Rabbi. The question is, what can I do about it?

I have good news for you.

You do?

If he couldn't answer your question, you won your choice of fresh fruit pie.

Yes, you see, fools never know they are fools. So if you know you're a fool, you must not really be one.

But everyone tells me I'm a fool.

And you believe what everyone tells you?

Sure, Rabbi.

Then perhaps you really are a fool.

So you're dreaming you're on a ship with your older brother and younger sister. The ship is sinking and you can save only one person besides yourself. What should you do?

Wake up.

There's this new rabbi in my town, and people are saying he can work all kinds of miracles. How can I tell if he's a fake?

This rabbi, does he claim he can stop you from thinking wicked thoughts?

Yes.

He's a fake.

BAD *BUBBE* TRIES AGAIN

The people went to the oil merchant's booth. Sure enough, she had fifty dollars in her money box.

I stand falsely accused, my friends. Unless you are accusing me of being the most brilliant saleswoman in the West.

Hand over that money before I get *really* mad.

Watch yourself, *Bubbe.*

I'm not your *bubbe.*

There's only one person who could possibly straighten this out.

On the other side of town:

Head down, knees bent, eyes on the ball ...

Fire it in here, Bernie! He can't touch it!

Rabbi Harvey was told he was needed to settle a dispute.

Just when I was really starting to drive the ball.

This sounds pretty simple. I'll be back by the time we take the field.

Take your time, Rabbi.

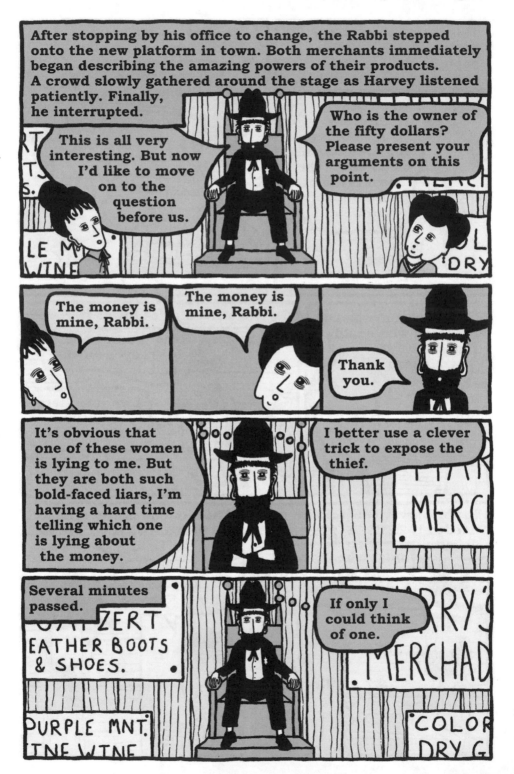

The crowd was getting restless.

How long is this going to take, Rabbi?

It's almost dinner time!

Yes, I am aware of that. But I just don't feel confident enough to make a ruling. And it's such a simple case. In addition, could the seat of this chair be any harder?

Let's go, Rabbi! I need to plant corn this weekend!

Boy, people can turn on you so quickly.

Well, don't panic, Harvey. Buy yourself a little time to think.

This case reminds me of a story. It seems that Yochanan ben Zakkai was walking with one of his students when—

Quit stalling, Rabbi!

He's pretending to be thirsty! That's the oldest trick in the book!

Yeah, quit your stalling, Rabbi!

Harvey insisted that he was not stalling.  The pitcher of water was brought. The Rabbi began dropping the coins into the water.

Have you ever tried to mix oil and water? If so, you've noticed that the oil, which is lighter than water, soon floats to the surface.

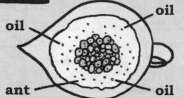

oil

oil

ant   oil

This is exactly what happened in the pitcher on Harvey's desk.

This is actually working. Remind me to buy you several pounds of chocolate.

I will. SPRING,

The Rabbi turned to the crowd.

Thank you all for your patience. As you can see, tiny beads of oil have lifted from the coins and are now floating on the surface of the water. It seems clear that whoever handled these coins had quite a bit of oil on her hands. Which leads me to conclude that—

The Rabbi was interrupted.

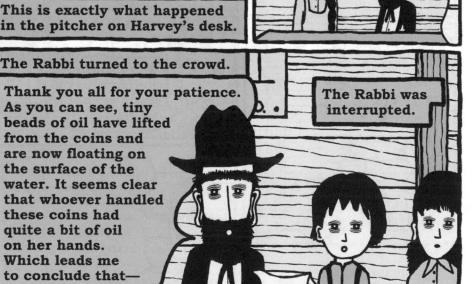

It was Tuesday, Rabbi Harvey's visiting day. He walked around Elk Spring, meeting with people who could not make it to his office.

Toward evening, the Rabbi stopped off at Sophie's house. Sophie had been sick in bed for almost a year.

There's someone here to see you, Sophie.

Send him in.

How are you feeling today?

Bored, Rabbi. Bored to death.

I could try another puppet show.

I don't know, Rabbi. You're not that good at doing the different voices. Everyone just sounds like you.

Perhaps that's true.

But you have not yet heard my fairly famous Abraham Lincoln impression.

This nation, under God, shall have a new birth of freedom! And government of the people, by the people, for the people shall not—

Sophie interrupted the president.

Um ... how about a story instead?

About what?

I don't care, Rabbi. But make it something real. Not made up.

Okay, let's go back ... way back to the olden days, when I first arrived in the West.

The truth is, I'm not really a professional baker. I've spent the last six years studying to be a rabbi.

Let's hope you're better at rabbi work than you are at making rolls.

Agreed.

Now, at this time, San Francisco had a very unusual mayor. He liked to put on disguises and walk around the streets unrecognized. This was his way of studying people — of learning things that he hoped would help him win elections.

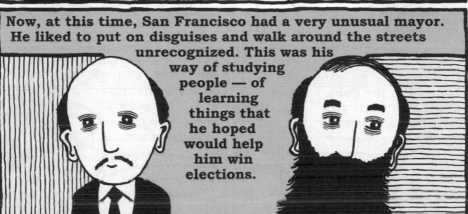

One day the mayor came to my roll cart. He was in disguise, so I didn't know it was him.

Greetings, young man! I'll take one of your fresh onion rolls.

So, how's the roll business these days?

Not bad, sir.

How long am I supposed to chew this thing before it begins to soften?

I'm curious, son. How much can a fellow like you earn in a day?

Oh, usually about a dollar.

That's all?

It's not much, I know. But I always seem to get by.

I see, but ... everyone else in California is rushing around searching for gold. I mean, don't you wish you had more money?

I wouldn't mind it, sir.

I've got everything I need for today, though. And as for tomorrow ... well, I'm sure something will turn up.

Interesting.

Later that evening, when the mayor was supposed to be thinking about the road construction budget:

I'm fascinated by that roll kid. I wonder how he'd respond if things got, well ... a little tougher for him?

The mayor thought up a little test.

NEW LAW!

BY ORDER OF THE MAYOR

ALL ROLL VENDORS MUST OBTAIN A LICENSE FROM THE CITY

COST: $20.⁰⁰

VIOLATORS WILL BE JAILED !!!

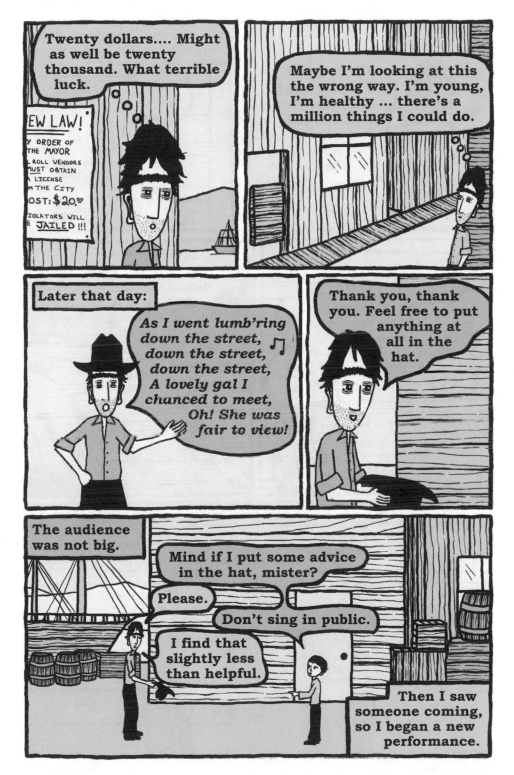

THE RABBI AND THE DRIVER

100

Rabbi Harvey and the young man went into the storeroom and had a long talk.

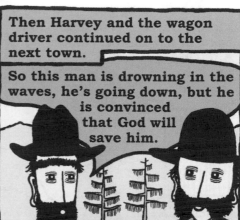

Then Harvey and the wagon driver continued on to the next town.

So this man is drowning in the waves, he's going down, but he is convinced that God will save him.

Soon a fishing boat sails up. But the drowning man refuses help. He insists that God will save him.

Finally the man drowns, he dies. And now he's really angry. He goes to God and demands: "What happened? Why didn't you save me?"

And God says, "You didn't see the boat?"

In the next town:

Shall we begin?

Later that afternoon, the Rabbi and the driver headed for the next town. This would be a new town on Harvey's circuit.

It must be an amazing feeling, Rabbi ...

To be greeted with such joy as you enter a town, to be welcomed and cheered and all.

It is a great honor. Lots of pressure, too.

I'm sure.

Still, I'd love to know what that felt like, just once. You know, to be the center of attention, hold the place of honor.

Several minutes later, in the town of Greene Gulch:

Here he comes, everybody!

Welcome to our town, Rabbi!

Hello! Thank you!

Nice to meet you!

The driver made his way through the adoring crowds.

Harvey carried the desk and chair from the wagon and set them up in town.

Shall we begin?

There was only one case in Greene Gulch, but it was a tricky one. The manager of the town bank handed over a copy of his father's will.

He died six months ago, Rabbi. And no one can figure out what his will means.

The driver read the brief document aloud.

"My son shall inherit all of my money and possessions. But not until he becomes foolish."

The Rabbi listened from his seat in the wagon.

What does it mean, Rabbi?

That's an excellent question.

I mean, to state the case in rather blunt terms ... when do I get my inheritance?

When, indeed?

Are you sure you're not already foolish?

Positive, Rabbi.

Go ahead, ask anyone. My father founded the bank here in town, and I practically grew up working there. He always taught me to be serious, sober, reliable, hard-working.

I see. That's good advice, of course.

Perhaps, uh, let me think ... what would the great rabbis of old have to say about this? Let's see, there was Rabbi, oh, what's his name? And the other one, with the hat....

Then, just as he was beginning to panic, the driver had an idea.

The truth is, sir, this is a very simple case.

It is?

It's so easy, my driver could solve it. Driver, come over here!

Who, me?

The Rabbi got down from the wagon. He leaned toward a woman in the crowd and asked an odd question.

I'm curious, ma'am. Have any of the families here in town recently had a baby?

He got the information he was looking for.

... then you'll see their house on the right side of the road.

Perfect, thank you.

Then he walked to the desk.

Why don't you go ahead and solve this one, driver?

I'll see what I can do.

Harvey asked the banker to follow him. He led the way to a small house on the edge of town.

He knocked on the door, and waited. There were strange sounds coming from inside the house.

Sounds like the right place.

ga ga shma shma shmeee shmeee shmoooooo!

Come in! shmeee shmeee, glaaglaahhh gleeeeee!

What a waste of time.

SPECIAL DELIVERY FROM RABBI HARVEY

It was another cold and snowy day in the Rocky Mountains.

In this small shack lived Otto and Edna. They were very poor and very hungry.

And very cold. Don't forget very cold.

They can see that, Otto.

I'm so sick of living like this.

We should do something about it.

You're right. Who can we complain to?

And I was wondering if you might ... if you weren't very busy ...

If you would, you know, like to ...

Boy, it's warm out here.

Just then something flew up and knocked off the Rabbi's hat.

Abigail suspected one of her students had thrown a snowball.

Come out from behind that tree, Louis!

But it was actually an envelope that had hit Harvey's hat.

The ink is a bit smeared by the snow, but it appears to be addressed to ... can that be right?

"... but they all fell into a river, and then we saved up and bought a bunch of turkeys, but they ate poison berries and died, and then ..."

Their claim, this company, is that they build their wagons from oak, ash, hickory — hardwoods native to the northeastern United States — and that, in contrast, companies out here rely primarily on western conifers, which are, as you know, classified as softwoods, and are, indeed, less dense

Yes, but—

in structure and less durable under many circumstances, which makes me wonder why factories around here don't consider ordering eastern timber, which would, of course, involve additional shipping costs, but then again, the eastern companies have to ship their entire wagons out here, which is expensive, and

The Rabbi went on talking and talking. Mrs. Zellerbach began to shiver. Soon she turned slightly blue.

... I would also consider birch an appropriate building material, and firmly support the use of elm, chestnut, certain types of cherry, maple, of course poplar—

Stop, Rabbi! I beg of you! If you love King David, stop talking!

This is all fascinating, I'm sure. But, Rabbi, I'm dying of cold out here.

I'm getting a bit cold myself. And we've only been standing outside for a few minutes.

STORY SOURCES

Rabbi Harvey Rides Again: A Graphic Novel of Jewish Wisdom Let Loose in the Wild West draws on thousands of years of Jewish teaching and storytelling.

Abigail v. the Wind

"Abigail v. the Wind" is adapted from a folktale set in the days of King Solomon. In the original story, a poor widow who lives by the sea sees her last loaf of bread carried off in a storm, and goes to Solomon to seek justice.

Wasserman and Son, ~~Barbers~~ Outlaws

The main plot of "Wasserman and Son, ~~Barbers~~ Outlaws" is based on a story told by the Hassidic master Rabbi Jacob Krantz of Dubno, in which a clever man takes advantage of his neighbor's greed. As Milt Wasserman tells the bartender, the question about "learning or action" comes from a Talmudic debate between Rabbi Tarfon and Rabbi Akiva.

The Rabbi's New Suit

"The Rabbi's New Suit" is based on a classic tale in which a man goes to a wedding—or fancy party of some kind, depending on the version—in old clothes, and gets ignored.

The Treasure Under the Pickles

Two stories are combined in "The Treasure Under the Pickles." The bit about the guy who sets out for the big city, gets turned around, and ends up back home without knowing it, is based on a Yiddish tale set in the legendary town of fools: Chelm. The story of the man who dreams of finding a treasure beneath a bridge in a far-off city comes from a famous tale by Rebbe Nachman of Breslov.

The Leadville Scavenger Hunt

"The Leadville Scavenger Hunt" makes use of a combination of folktales. The story about the tear of the repentant thief is based on a tale in which a disobedient angel is given the opportunity to redeem himself by finding the most valuable thing in the world. The trick Harvey uses to waste the bandit's bullets comes from a story in which a Jew uses similar strategies to outwit a robber.

Stump the Rabbi

Harvey calls on teachings from many sources in "Stump the Rabbi." For example, the "Am I rich?" question comes from a Talmudic tale in which Alexander the Great asks the wise men in Jerusalem, "Who is rich?" To which they reply, "He who is happy with what he has." The gem about how to tell if a self-promoting rabbi is genuine is based on a teaching of the Baal Shem Tov. Another Hassidic teaching, this time from The Maggid of Mezeritch, provides Harvey with his response to the couple that comes to him desperate to have a child.

Bad *Bubbe* Tries Again

"Bad *Bubbe* Tries Again" adapts a classic tale of a robbery, oil, coins, and the wisdom of a child. Also thrown in is a detail from a Talmudic tale in which a town builds a fancy platform for its rabbi, only to have the rabbi's wisdom suddenly leave him while he is sitting on the stage.

Deputy Harvey: San Francisco Police

An ancient Jewish tale from Afghanistan forms the basis for "Deputy Harvey: San Francisco Police." The original pits a poor man against a curious Shah who likes to disguise himself and walk among his people.

The Rabbi and the Driver

"The Rabbi and the Driver" makes use of another tale by Jacob Krantz of Dubno, one in which a rabbi and driver change places. The puzzling will comes from a story in the Talmud told about Rabbi Joshua ben Korha, whose joy with his own baby son provides the key to the riddle.

Special Delivery from Rabbi Harvey

"Special Delivery from Rabbi Harvey" combines two tales of rabbis who pry donations from misers, while teaching them lessons at the same time. The tale of the poor couple's letter to God, and their suspicion of the generous soul who responds, is also adapted from a classic folktale.

SUGGESTIONS FOR FURTHER READING

Ausubel, Nathan, ed. *A Treasury of Jewish Folklore*. New York: Crown Publishers, 1989.

Kaplan, Aryeh, trans. *The Lost Princess & Other Kabbalistic Tales of Rebbe Nachman of Breslov*. Woodstock, VT: Jewish Lights, 2005.

———. *The Seven Beggers & Other Kabbalistic Tales of Rebbe Nachman of Breslov*. Woodstock, VT: Jewish Lights, 2005.

*Katchor, Ben. *Julius Knipl: Real Estate Photographer*. Boston: Little, Brown and Company, 1996.

*Mack, Stan. *The Story of the Jews: A 4,000-Year Adventure—A Graphic History Book*. Woodstock, VT: Jewish Lights, 2001.

*Modan, Rutu. *Exit Wounds*. Montreal: Drawn & Quarterly, 2007.

Rochlin, Fred and Harriet. *Pioneer Jews: A New Life in the Far West*. Boston: Houghton Mifflin, 2000.

*Sfar, Joann. *Klezmer: Tales of the Wild East*. New York: First Second, 2006.

Sheinkin, David. *Path of the Kabbalah*. New York: Paragon House, 1986.

*Sheinkin, Steve. *The Adventures of Rabbi Harvey: A Graphic Novel of Jewish Wisdom and Wit in the Wild West*. Woodstock, VT: Jewish Lights, 2006.

*———. *Rabbi Harvey vs. the Wisdom Kid: A Graphic Novel of Dueling Jewish Folktales in the Wild West*. Woodstock, VT: Jewish Lights, 2010.

*Spiegelman, Art. *Maus: A Survivor's Tale: My Father Bleeds History / Here My Troubles Began*. New York: Pantheon, 1991.

*Waldman, JT. *Megillat Esther*. Philadelphia: Jewish Publication Society, 2006.

Wiesel, Elie. *Souls on Fire: Portraits and Legends of Hasidic Masters*. New York: Simon & Schuster, 1982.

* graphic novels / comics